FOR M

FO YOU,
THE AMAZING
BRAVE SOUL,
THE STUDENT OF
MAGIC ARTS

© 2018 Catherine Fet

North Landing Books

Definitions

What are spells, charms, and divination?

Spell

A spell is words and actions that have magic powers.

Charm

Charms are spells that change an object without turning it into a different object. For instance, giving water healing power is a charm.

Divination

Divination is seeking knowledge of the future by means of magical arts. In a divination you ask a question, and magic forces of the universe answer it.

Remember

• It's ok to read the spells, you don't have to remember them by heart.

• You can write a journal of the spells you do, so you can track the results, and work on improving your magic skills.

• Share your magic work with your family, and teach them respectfully about the goals of your magic and how it grows your knowledge and makes the world better.

Before I share with you
the secret knowledge I have received from my family,
and gained through years of my own magic training,
I am bound by a pledge to ask of you the same.

Please put your hand on your heart and say:

I PROMISE TO HARM NO ONE
WITH MY KNOWLEDGE, MY WILL,
MY SPELLWORK, OR MY SILENCE.

REMEMBER

YOUR MAGIC WAND

You can make a magic wand yourself,
or buy it, or receive it as a gift.

If you make a wand from a fresh tree branch, remember
that each wand has a top and a bottom, so make sure
the branch is not upside down. Like tree sap,
the magic energy will flow up your wand.
Wands often have a stone at the top to direct
and radiate magic energy.
Another way to direct it is to decorate your wand with
a spiral going up in a clockwise direction. It can be wire,
thread, ribbon, or paint. You can use a string of beads
with colors that have a special meaning to you.

Clockwise:
in the same direction
as the hands of a clock.

Counter-clockwise:
the opposite direction

Remember: when you start looking for a magic wand,

YOUR WAND FINDS YOU

The magic forces of the universe respond to your
intention to make the wand, and send ideas and materials
for the wand your way.

To check if your wand is working, hold it in your
dominant hand: If you are right-handed - in your right hand,
and if you are left-handed - in your left hand, and point it
to the palm of your other hand (about 2 inches away).
If you feel tingling or warmth in
the palm of your hand,
the energy is flowing.

Consecration

To make the wand truly yours, you need to consecrate it.
Consecrate your wand by filling it with your intention
and with the power of your will.

Consecration of the wand is a ritual of commanding your wand
to serve you. The word "consecration" comes from the Latin
"sacer" which means "sacred, holy."
In ancient Grece, they believed that the world was made of
natural elements: Earth, Water, Air, and Fire.
We follow this tradition, calling the four elements
to be witnesses in our ritual.

Make a beautiful circle of any material you like -
leaves, flowers, beads, marbles, or stones. You can also draw
this circle, and fill it with pictures and words that have
a special meaning to you. Place your wand in the middle.
Holding your hand over it, say these words:

By the power of the elements,
Earth, Water, Air, and Fire,
I consecrate this wand
to carry my will
beyond matter
and spirit.

Rain Water Spell

A spell to get a person you know to help you or be on your side.

To cast this spell you will need

a small mirror
rain water
a stalk of grass, a twig, or a small stick
a bowl
flower petals
your magic wand

Use the twig/stick to write the name of the person
whose help you are seeking on the mirror
with rain water. Wave your magic wand
slowly over the mirror saying:

I bind you left, I bind you right,
Be on my side day and night.

Take the mirror and drop it
into the bowl of water, saying:

Rain and ocean are one
Under the moon and the sun.

Now throw flower petals into the bowl, saying:

From me to you
Good will times two.

Make sure that, floating on the water,
flower petals cover all the water
surface in the bowl.

THE THREE LEAVES DIVINATION

This ancient divination ritual reveals who is thinking of you right now.

To perform this divination you will need

a bowl
3 green leaves
1 small white stone
sea water, or tap water and a pinch of salt
your magic wand

Fill the bowl with sea water (or use tap water mixed with salt).
Put it in a place where half of the bowl
is in the sun and the other half is in the shade.
Toss the white stone into the bowl saying:
Stone cold tell the sea
Who is thinking now of me...

Toss the first green leaf into the bowl.
Hold your magic wand over the bowl, saying:
Wind tells its secrets to the tree,
It grows wise, it grows free,
I request of it three leaves
To be used by me.

Toss the second green leaf into the bowl.
Hold your magic wand over the bowl, saying:
The roots are deep
The tree is tall,
The leaves see everything,
They know all.

Toss the third green leaf into the bowl.
Hold your magic wand over the bowl, saying:
Ocean deep can its secrets keep
But the leaves tell me all
As in the waves they fall.

Now hold your magic wand in front of your face, and
quickly close your eyes. In the darkness, the magic wand will show
you the person who is thinking of you. Use the Friend or Foe spell
to find out if they are your friend — or your enemy

THE POLAR STAR CHARM

*The **North Star, Polar Star, or Polaris** was believed by ancient people to stand still in the sky while other stars circled around. It became a symbol of loyalty.*
How to find Polaris: Find the constellation of the Big Dipper. Connect two stars in the bowl of the Big Dipper with an imaginary line, and continue this line about five times the height of the dipper bowl. The bright star at the end of the line is Polaris.

This charm is believed to give you courage and strength by calling on the eternal loyalty of the North Star.

You will need:
a crystal, or a pendant on a cord, or a necklace
a tall glass
On a clear night you will need to find the North Star.

Fill the glass with water, take it outside, where you can see the Polar Star. Hold your pendant or necklace in front of you, and, with your eyes on the Star, say:
Give me courage, give me love
As lasting as your light above.

Drop the necklace into the glass with these words:
Accept my heart, and keep the key.
As is my will so let it be.
Drink the water with the necklace still in the glass.
From now on, this necklace is a key that belongs to Polaris.
Touch it any time, you need strength and courage.

"Harm No One" Spell

Also known as the "Thunderstorm Spell" this magic ritual should be performed when a storm or other danger comes near your home.

To cast this spell you will need
a bottle of water
an offering of food (a few seeds, nuts, or fruit)
flowers
your magic wand

Put the bottle of water on the ground outside.
Place food and flowers around it.
This food offering is a symbol of your good will
toward the forces of the universe, known and unknown.

A SYMBOL is an object or a sign that stands for something you can't see with your eyes, such as an idea or a feeling. GOOD WILL is a feeling of approval and support.

Sit for a minute next to your offering, and if you feel fear, quietly tell it to leave your heart. Stand up, raise your magic wand up toward the storm clouds, and say:

The magic of black, go back.
The magic of white, bring me the light.

Seal your spell by pouring water from the bottle
on the ground 4 times. Pour and say:
On count 1 my spell's begun.

Pour again, saying: On count 2 it will come true.

Pour the third time, saying: On count 3, winds, obey me.

Change the words of the spell if necessary.
If the danger you want to stop is fire,
you will say On count 3, fire, obey me.
If it's a volcano, say: On count 3, volcano, obey me.

Pour the fourth time, saying: On count four, harm us no more.
Throw your food offering on the wind, let it fly away.

Serpent Inside

Grow your magic power: Charge your magic wand. Learn about the phases of the Moon. It takes the Moon about 29 and a half days to complete all its phases, from new Moon to new Moon.

Find out the date of the next full moon.
On the night of the full moon
charge your magic wand
by leaving it in the moonlight overnight -
indoors or outdoors.

If it's cloudy and the moon is not visible,
you will have to wait till next month.

As you place your wand in the moonlight,
say these magic words:

Serpent inside!
Drink of the moonlight.
Bring its power to me,
I will set you free.

Phases of the Moon

new   young   waxing crescent   waxing quarter   waxing gibbou

full   waning gibbous   waning quarter   waning crescent   old

THREE TIMES THREE

Grow your magic power: recharge your intuition.

*INTUITION is the ability to know things without being told.
Everyone has some intuition, but skilled
magicians' intuition is so powerful,
they can often see into the future, and predict
future events. Deepen your intuition with this spell
that binds you to the knowledge pathways of the universe.*

You will need:

a feather
a piece of thread or ribbon

You will need to know the four cardinal directions
that is the directions of North, South, East and West.
You can use a compass to find them.

Tie the feather to the end of a thread
or a ribbon, and let it
fly in the wind.

Establish from which direction
the wind is blowing.
If it blows from the East,
face the East,
bow and address the wind
with these words:

My Lord, East wind,
Leave no secrets behind.
Three times three
Bring them to me.

Check the direction of the wind from time to time
over days or weeks, and ask all 4 winds
to share their knowledge with you.
Make sure you ask each wind for help 3 times,
and the wind will return to you "three times three"
with its gifts to grow your wisdom.

THE SALT CIRCLE SPELL

This is a breaking spell. It breaks any spell cast against you.

You will need:
a plate
a wine glass
salt
pen and paper

Pour salt onto a plate and shape it into a circle using the base of a wine glass. Pour water into the glass and place it inside the salt circle.
If you know the name of a person who cast a spell against you write their name on a piece of paper. If you don't know who cast the spell, but you can tell there is a spell working against you, give a name to the spell cast against you.
For instance, if you are sad without a reason, and you think it's a result of a spell, call it Sadness Spell. Write it down.
Drop the piece of paper with the name of the person or spell into the glass, and pour salt on top of it. Say these magic word.

Pure heart, lift the curse,
Any loss be reversed.
Pure salt, break the spell
Make me whole, make me well.

Dig a hole under a tree, bury the
paper with your writing in the ground,
and pour the water from the glass
over it.

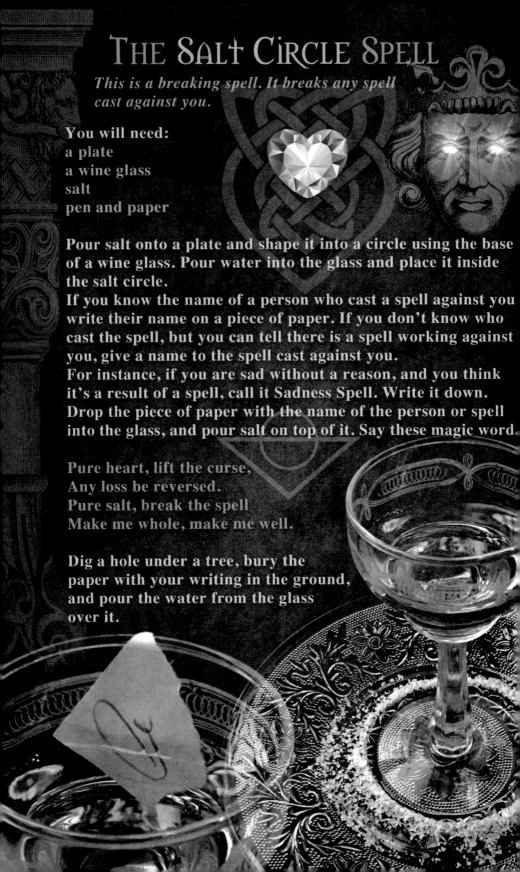

Pendulum Divination (1)

A pendulum is an object that swings freely hanging from a fixed point. Pendulums have been used for divination for thousands of years. This is a very ancient magical art.

You will need:
a pendulum
a glass + cold and hot water
white salt, white sugar

Make a pendulum out of a simple metal or stone object you can tie to a thread, a string, or a chain. It can be a ring, a stone, a bead, or even a paperclip. The string or chain should be about 5 inches (or 12 centimeters) long.

Clean your pendulum of any bad energy by keeping it for 1 minute in a glass of cold water mixed with salt, and for 1 minute in hot water mixed with sugar.

Sit comfortably and lift your pendulum. Let it rest for a moment on the palm of your other hand, and say these words in Latin:

<u>Semper ad meliora (mey-lee-O-rah)</u>
which means: Always for the best

Now lift the pendulum into the air making sure it's hanging still, and say: Pendulum, show me a yes.
Wait till the pendulum starts swinging
(it may take from a few seconds to a few minutes, so be patient!) and notice the pattern of its movement. Maybe it's side-to-side, or in a circle. Also notice the direction of its movement.

Now lower the pendulum onto the palm of your hand again, let it rest and say these words in Latin:

<u>Semper nox</u> which mean: Always night.

Lift the pendulum into the air gently.
Check that it's hanging still and say: Pendulum, show me a no.

Again, notice the pattern and direction of its movement.
Now you can try asking your pendulum your divination questions. These may be questions about future events, or about people you know.

Remember

Never use your pendulum when
you are upset or frustrated.

Perform this divination only for yourself,
never for another person.

Use the pendulum to seek hidden knowledge
but not to make decisions.

Don't let anyone touch it.
If anyone but you touches it,
you will need to clean it again.

Store it close to the place where you sleep,
best of all under your pillow.

Latin

Latin is a language that was spoken in
Ancient Rome. Ancient Roman civilization
lasted between the 7th century BC and
the 5th century AD.

BC means "Before Christ,"
AD stands for Latin words
"Anno Domini" (doh-mee-nee)
which means "the year of the Lord,"
because our calendar counts years
from the birth of Jesus Christ.

Later, in the Middle Ages
(which lasted from 500 AD to 1500 AD)
Latin became the language of church service
science, books, and magical arts.
Many magic spells came to us
from Ancient Rome and the Middle Ages.

*Statue of a
Roman emperor
in Rome, Italy*

NUMEROLOGY (1)

Numerology is a type of divination that studies number patterns to find hidden knowledge and predict future events.

YOUR LIFE PATH NUMBER

Add up the numbers in the **day, month, and year of your birth.**
If it's November 10, 2011 (11/10/2011), add: 1+1+1+0+2+0+1+1=7
If the sum is a 2-digit number, like 12, make it 1 digit like this: 1+2=3
So your number is 3. If the sum is a Master number, 11 or 22,
don't turn it into 1 digit! Then look at the list below to see
the life path predicted by your birthday number.

MEANINGS OF LIFE PATH NUMBERS in NUMEROLOGY

1 leader and innovator, pure positive energy
2 influencer with deep intuition and knowledge of people
3 high energy multi-talented creative achiever
4 the one who gets the job done: focus, motivation + best skills
5 fast thinker, world traveler, master communicator
6 leader and peacemaker, caring family person
7 scholar, seeker of wisdom, or a master of magic
8 great willpower and success in business
9 intellectual achievement, courage and kindness
11 visionary with spiritual knowledge, and ability to inspire others
22 power and influence of a master builder and teacher

CURRENT YEAR PREDICTION NUMBER

Add up your **Life Path Number** and the number of the current year:
If your Life Path number is 7 and the year is 2019:
7+2+0+1+9=19 Turn 2-digit numbers into 1 digit: 1+9=10, 1+0=1

THE MEANING OF CURRENT YEAR NUMBERS

1 expect great new opportunities coming your way this year
2 expect to find new friends this year
3 expect success + secrets will be revealed
4 the year of hope, hard work, and slow steady progress
5 the year of big changes in your neighborhood, city, or country
6 a good year for your family and family members
7 expect a lot of progress in school
8 this year you will be recognized for your achievements
9 expect changes in yourself - more wisdom and responsibility

Numerology (2)

Numerology is a magic art that studies number patterns to gain hidden knowledge and predict future events.

YOUR NAME NUMBER

Add up the numbers corresponding to the letters in your name, using this chart:

1	2	3	4	5	6	7	8	9
A	B	C	D	E	F	G	H	I
J	K	L	M	N	O	P	Q	R
S	T	U	V	W	X	Y	Z	

Here is how I calculate the number for my name:
Catherine = 3+1+2+8+5+9+9+5+5=47>4+7>**11** (master number)
Fet = 6+5+2=13>1+3>**4**
11+4=15>1+5>**6**

6 means that I am a leader, a peacemaker, and
a caring family member, and, you know, it's absolutely true!!!

Look at the **MEANINGS OF LIFE PATH NUMBERS** list
on the previous page to interpret the meaning of your name number.

They say that in the Western world
Numerology was first taught by
ancient Greek mathematician
Pythagoras who lived in the
6th century BC. Pythagoras believed
that number 1 represented the creation
of the world, and the number 2 represented all the
things in the world. He also taught that number 3 was
a perfect number, because it had a beginning (1),
a middle (2), and an end (3).

SACRED GEOMETRY

Geometry is a branch of mathematics that studies geometrical figures, such as triangles, circles, and squares.
Sacred geometry looks for the sacred geometric patterns and laws deep in the heart of our universe.

THE PYTHAGOREAN THEOREM

Learn one of the laws of sacred geometry, laid down by Pythagoras.
Use it to demand the cosmic order give way to your magic.
A THEOREM is a rule, or a principle in math.

Pythagoras' theorem says that in a triangle with a right angle the square of its long side is the same as the squares of its other 2 sides put together. Number 2 over A,B,C mean "square."

$$A^2 + B^2 = C^2$$

C

A

B

triangle

right angle

not a right angle

Ancient magicians believed that this rule is one of the secret foundations of the world. Many ancient structures, such as the great pyramids of Egypt were built using this principle.

Here is a spell to make your magic wand, especially a new one, precise, like the Pythagorean Theorem.
On a clear night, lift your magic wand to the sky and draw a triangle in the air. Make sure it has a right angle. Use the picture above to remember which sides are A, B and C. Now point to the sides of this imaginary triangle and say:

My magic wand draws in the air
A square and B square.
Together they equal square C.
The door is open, I have the key.

C

A

B

Magic Symbols of Ancient Egypt

Ancient Egyptians often drew the sun god Ra with a head of a falcon, with the sun on his head, and a cobra snake around the sun disk. In his right hand Ra holds the Ankh. Egyptians believed it was a symbol of life, and used it in magic. They also believed that every day Ra, the Sun crossed the sky in a boat, and then went down into the underworld (the world of the dead) at night

Another magic symbol of the sun in Ancient Egypt was a scarab (an oval beetle), always shown in Egyptian art with a sun disk.

And you need to know one more symbol of Egyptian magic: the Eye of Horus

This eye is a symbol of protection and royal power.

Solar Breath Spell

Does it happen to you that you are upset, or angry,
you want to scream, you don't know what to say or do?..
When it happens to me, I use this ancient Egyptian spell
to clear my mind, and give me strength to radiate truth
and power in every word I say.

Solar means "from the sun"

To perform this spell you will need:
a mirror (a hand-held or a wall mirror)
a name for yourself using the word "sun," or "solar," or "Ra"
a napkin
Ancient Egyptians believed that the sun god, Ra, created
all forms of life on Earth by calling their secret names.
Give yourself a secret name that only you and the sun know.
It can be "Son of the Solar Wind," or "Daughter of the Sun,"
any name that connects you to the ancient sun magic.

Go to a quiet place where nobody can see you. Take a mirror
(or you can use a wall mirror), breathe on the mirror until it
fogs up, and draw on the fog this Egyptian sun hieroglyph.

hieroglyph = hai-ro-glif

Now fix your eyes on this sun symbol, and
do the magic breathing called the Four-Fold Breath:
Inhale for a count of four. Hold your breath for a count of four.
Exhale for a count of four. Hold your breath for a count of four.
Repeat if you can still clearly see the sun sign on the mirror.
Once the sign has faded, wipe the mirror clean.
Your ritual is done.

Why does your breath fog up the mirror?
Your breath has water in it, in the form of vapor. When it hits
the cold mirror, the water "condenses" that is, turns into tiny droplets
on the mirror, because the cooler the air, the less vapor it can hold.

Instead of using letters to write,
Ancient Egyptians used hieroglyphs,
which means pictures of objects.
For instance,
this hieroglyph
means "a house."
This one means
a town.

Cosmic Order

From ancient times the goal of magic arts has been to learn about the secret laws and patterns of the universe, or the Cosmic Order, and to use them in magic. As a student of magic, you must learn to recognize these sacred principles of the Cosmic Order, and to use them in your magic practice.

Sacred Symmetry

One of the patterns observed in nature is Symmetry. A symmetrical object is the same on both sides, like a mirror's reflection. Or maybe it's the same at the top and at the bottom. Butterflies are symmetrical, and so are most living things. Your face and body are symmetrical.

When you are preparing objects and tools for a magic spell, use symmetry to connect with the Cosmic Order.

Here is a Sacred Symmetry power charm that calls on the creative energy at the core of the universe to give you powers, such as strength, patience, or wisdom to achieve your goal.

PATIENCE

Put a sheet of paper in a place where it's half in the light and half in the shade. Put any 2 objects that look alike at the top. Write the same symbol (any symbol) on both sides. Now, on the right write the word that describes what power you need now.

Next, touch here with your magic wand, and say these words in Latin: Symmetria divina, semper fidelis (Symmetry divine, always true).

Fractals and Spirals

In math fractals are patterns that repeat again and again. Fractals and spirals are everywhere in nature, and are part of the sacred geometry of the universe. Fractals and spirals can multiply and grow endlessly. Learn to use their power! This will help you increase the reach of your magic.

Fractals in broccoli: If you look closely at the smallest piece of this type of broccoli, you will see that it looks exactly like a bigger chunk. The fractals repeat growing smaller, and smaller, and smaller, or larger, and larger, and larger!

Fractals in a seashell: The spiral pattern is repeating itself as the shell grows. The biggest known spirals are star galaxies.

Fibonacci Sequence

The best spiral for magic is based on numbers we call the Fibonacci numbers: 1, 1, 2, 3, 5, 8, 13 and so on, where each number is the sum of the two previous numbers: 1+1=2, 1+2=3, 2+3=5, 3+5=8, 5+8=13, 13+8=21... If your spell is based on these numbers, your magic power grows fast, and reaches very far, like the spiral of a galaxy. On the next page, we'll learn how to make a special tool to use the power of spirals that are based on Fibonacci numbers.

Rose petals, and the shell of the Nautilus mollusk grow following the Fibonacci sequence. With every turn the spiral gets wider, and travels farther from its center.

Spiral Charm

*Fibonacci (fee-bo-nAh-chi) was an Italian mathematician
who lived in the Middle Ages, in the 13th century. He started using
Arabic numerals (the numbers we use now!) instead of Roman
numerals that were used in Europe at that time. Compare:*
Arabic numerals: 1, 2, 3, 5, 10, 50
Roman numerals: I, II, III, V, X, L

To make a Fibonacci spiral magic tool, based on the Fibonacci
numbers, use graph paper (square grid), or make your own
using a ruler: 8 squares high and 13 squares long.

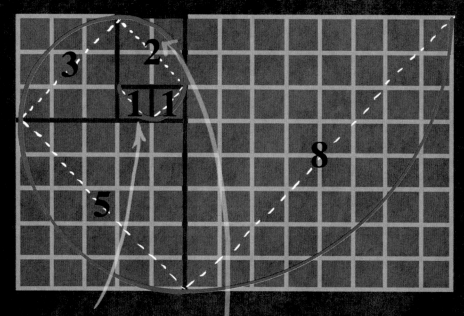

Find the first 2 squares, and mark them with the number 1.
Now start drawing the spiral, crossing these squares diagonally.
Diagonally means from corner to corner up or down.
Next find the 4 squares above 1 and 1, and mark them 2.
This next piece of your spiral will be 2 squares wide.
I draw the diagonal line first (corner to corner in white dots),
then I draw the spiral above it (in red). Your next piece of spiral is
5 squares wide, and the last one will be 8 squares wide.
When doing magic, you can always finish any spell with this
spiral charm to multiply the power of your magic indefinitely.
Say these words as you follow the spiral with the tip of your
magic wand:
On 1 my spiral will arise. On 2 it's fire. On 3 it's ice.
On 5 it's a serpent. On 8 it's a star.
My will be done, wherever you are.

THE BLACK STONE SPELL

This spell will make any person tell you a secret

To cast this spell you will need
a small black stone
a hammer, a shovel
a napkin or a piece of fabric
a teaspoonful of sugar
your magic wand

Hold your magic wand in your hand. Close your eyes
and imagine the person who hides something from you
standing in front of you. Point your magic wand
to their heart, saying:
I will use my magic art
To open the secrets of your heart.
If your heart is like a stone,
All its secrets will be known.

Put the black stone on a hard surface outside, such as a sidewalk.
Make sure it's in the shade. Wave your magic wand
over it, saying:
Stone cold, stone black
Tell me your secret,
Don't hold back.

Pour some sugar over the stone, saying:
Take my gift, take my treat
Spill your secret nice and sweet.

Close your eyes again and focus on the person you imagine standing
in front of you. If they nod their head, your spell is done,
and they will likely tell you their secret next time you see them.
If there is no nod, cover the stone with a napkin,
then take a hammer in your hand, and say:

I'll break the bind so I may find
That secret deep inside your mind.

Break the stone with a hammer, and use the shovel to bury
the pieces of the stone in the ground. This last spell is sure to work.

Three Silver Coins Spell

A spell to make the secret tunnels and doors of the universe guide you in a difficult task

To cast this spell you will need
3 silver-toned coins
a key

Throw 3 coins outside, as far as you can, saying:

Take my gifts,
Earth, water, air
Help me
Guide me
Treat me fair.

Don't look for the coins, and if they fall
somewhere where you can see them,
let them be lost, or let someone else find them.

Put the key on the palm of your right hand,
lift it up, and look into the sky, saying:

Star fire, mold me a key
To open air, land, and sea.

Now close your eyes and picture
7 stars coming together into a constellation
(a constellation is a group of stars that forms a shape)
making the shape of a key like the one you hold in your hand.
With your eyes closed, imagine your hand
taking that key, and say:

Open doors
Above and below
Let me fly, let me flow.

With the ancient gates of the hidden world open to you,
and the magic energy of the sky and the earth in your hand,
expect faster progress in whatever you are working on.

THE DARK WAVE SPELL

This spell will make an angry person calm down

To cast this spell you will need

a glass of water
green leaves
flower petals
a shovel
your magic wand

Put green leaves in a circle on a table or on the floor.
Shake the glass, so that a bit of water spills out, and put it in the
middle of the circle. Point your magic wand at it, saying:

Dark wave go away
Clear sky is here to stay.

Think of one secret word that describes the angry person's
transformation, like "happy", or "friendly."
Throw flower petals into the glass, saying:

I make you calm
I bring you peace
My word will make
Your anger cease.

Now pour the water with the flower petals outside near
a growing tree, and repeat your secret word 3 times.

Turn toward the tree and say:

Be my witness, silent tree
My will be done times three.

Finally, bury the green leaves under the tree using the shovel.

If there is a person you want to stay away from you, use

THE • BANISH FOREVER • SPELL

To cast this spell you will need

a little bit of milk
a small stick, or a twig
a white sheet of paper
you also need to know where North, South,
East, and West are.

Dip the twig in milk, and use milk to write
the person's name, or initials (first letters of their first and
last names) on the sheet of paper.
As the letters vanish, repeat:
White on white
Out of my sight
On count four
I close the door.

Fold the paper into fourths (fold in half, and again in half),
then tear the paper into 4 pieces.

Draw a compass star (arrows indicating 4 directions, like this).
Rotate (turn) the picture, so it matches North, South, East, West.

Put each of the 4 pieces of
paper you tore at the 4 tips
of the compass star, and say:

Four winds take you away.
Never come back night or day.

Take the remaining milk outside,
and bury it in the ground.
Once it's buried, say these words out loud:

Into the ground,
Forever bound,
You can't be found,
You're not around.

Stones of Three Divination

A divination to help you figure out whether to act or to wait.
This ancient art of divination by casting stones is called Lithomancy.

To perform this divination you will need
3 small stones or beads
wine glass half filled with milk
A spoon

On a sheet of white paper, draw three overlapping circles.
Bind these circles to your magic art by writing the first letter
of your name in the middle of each circle.

Say these words in Latin "Omne trium perfectum"
(a set of three is complete).

Put a stone in each circle and say:
Stones of three, guide me.

Place the glass with milk in the middle so it covers
the area where the circles intersect.
Cast the 3 stones into the glass so they are completely
covered with milk. Then, dip a spoon into the glass,
close your eyes, and ask your question.
Wait, allow the magical energy to flow around and within you.

Now scoop the stones and the milk with the spoon, eyes closed,
lift the spoon over the glass, and open your eyes.
What is in the spoon?
• If it's just milk - don't act, just wait
• 1 stone on the spoon, seek more knowledge about
the matter and prepare for action
• 2 stones - commit to act at some point in the future
• 3 stones - don't wait too long, act soon.

Leave the milk in the glass overnight, and in the morning
pour the milk outside near a growing tree.

You can repeat this divination every few days or even every day
if your situation or your feelings about it change.

Water and Oil Divination

This form of divination comes from ancient Babylon. It was often used to find out if a person you know is "friend or foe."

To perform this divination you will need
a small bowl or glass of water
some clear oil, like vegetable cooking oil

Lift the oil container over the bowl of water and pour oil into the water slowly noticing the patterns the oil makes on the water's surface.
If the oil forms filled circular shapes, the answer to your question is likely to be positive. If the oil spreads in droplets and forms many disconnected shapes instead of one larger shape, the answer to your question is likely to be negative.

An additional test is to toss a coin into the water with oil floating on top. Did the coin break the oil shape into smaller shapes? If yes, again, the anwer to your question may be negative.
In Ancient Babylon they also believed that if the oil made a crescent moon shape, it's a very good sign, indicating good luck for you and your family.

Why do oil and water never mix?
Every substance has its own density.
Oil is less dense than water,
so it always floats to the top.

Crescent moon...
The word "crescent"
comes from Latin
"crescere" = to grow

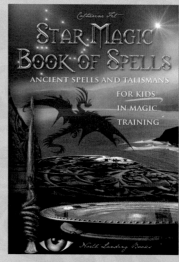

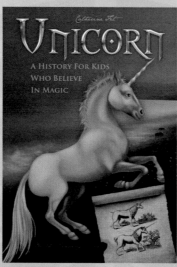

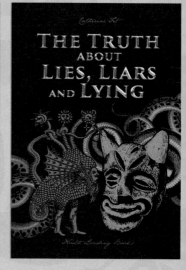

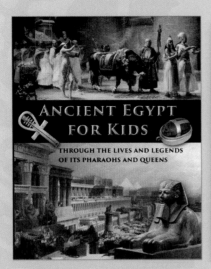

ANCIENT EGYPT FOR KIDS

THROUGH THE LIVES AND LEGENDS OF ITS PHARAOHS AND QUEENS

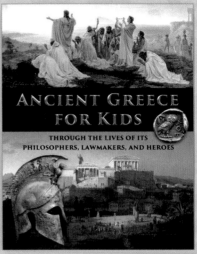

ANCIENT GREECE FOR KIDS

THROUGH THE LIVES OF ITS PHILOSOPHERS, LAWMAKERS, AND HEROES

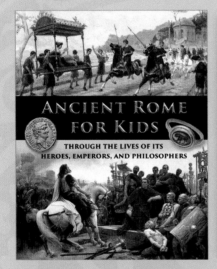

ANCIENT ROME FOR KIDS

THROUGH THE LIVES OF ITS HEROES, EMPERORS, AND PHILOSOPHERS

THE MIDDLE AGES FOR KIDS

THROUGH THE LIVES OF KINGS, HEROES, AND SAINTS

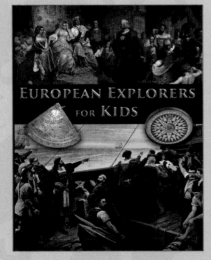

EUROPEAN EXPLORERS FOR KIDS

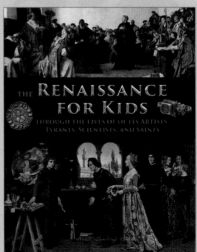

THE RENAISSANCE FOR KIDS

THROUGH THE LIVES OF OF ITS ARTISTS, TYRANTS, SCIENTISTS, AND SAINTS

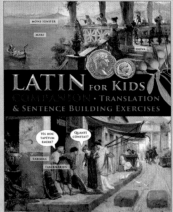

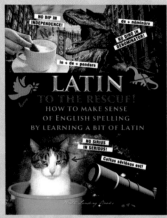

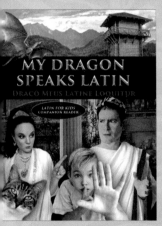

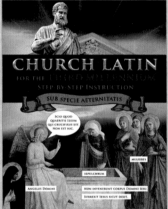

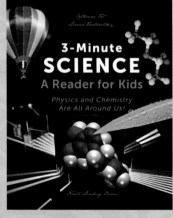

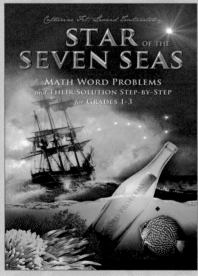

Catherine Fet

READING ALONE **2**

TREASURE HUNTING

AND REAL LIFE TREASURE HUNTERS

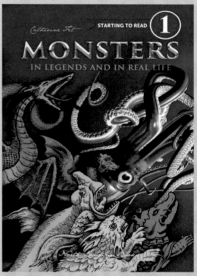

Catherine Fet

STARTING TO READ **1**

MONSTERS

IN LEGENDS AND IN REAL LIFE

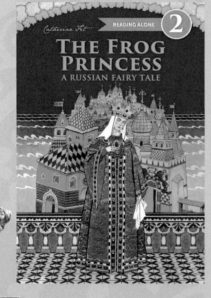

Catherine Fet

READING ALONE **2**

THE FROG PRINCESS

A RUSSIAN FAIRY TALE

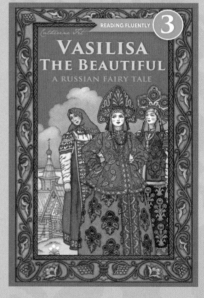

Catherine Fet

READING FLUENTLY **3**

VASILISA THE BEAUTIFUL

A RUSSIAN FAIRY TALE

Made in the USA
Las Vegas, NV
18 December 2023

83114154R00021